FELICITY'S DANCING SHOES

FELICITY · 1774

BY VALERIE TRIPP

ILLUSTRATIONS DAN ANDREASEN

VIGNETTES SUSAN MCALILEY

THE AMERICAN GIRLS COLLECTION®

Published by Pleasant Company Publications
Previously published in *American Girl*® magazine
© Copyright 2000 by Pleasant Company

For information, address: Book Editor, Pleasant Company Publications,
8400 Fairway Place, P.O. Box 620998, Middleton, WI 53562.

·
Printed in Singapore.
00 01 02 03 04 05 06 07 TWP 10 9 8 7 6 5 4 3 2 1

Edited by Camela Decaire, Nancy Holyoke, and Michelle Jones
Designed by Laura Moberly and Kimberly Strother
Art Directed by Kym Abrams and Kimberly Strother

Library of Congress Cataloging-in-Publication Data

Tripp, Valerie, 1951-
Felicity's dancing shoes / by Valerie Tripp ; illustrations,
Dan Andreasen ; vignettes, Susan McAliley.
p. cm. — (The American girls collection)
Summary: In colonial Williamsburg, nine-year-old Felicity's dancing
skills improve when she changes from wearing clumsy shoes to dainty
slippers but ultimately she learns that "Gracefulness is in the foot, not the shoe."
Includes information on the education of girls in colonial America, focusing
on dance, and presents square dance instructions.

ISBN 1-58485-031-0
[1. Dance Fiction. 2. Shoes Fiction. 3. Williamsburg (Va.)—History Fiction.
4. United States — Social life and customs — To 1775 Fiction.]
I. Andreasen, Dan, ill. II. Title. III. Series.
PZ7.T7363Fekh 2000   [Fic]—dc21   99-38624 CIP

OTHER AMERICAN GIRLS
SHORT STORIES:

PICTURE CREDITS

The following organizations have generously given permission to reprint illustrations contained in "Looking Back": p. 30—Philip and Charlotte Hanes; p. 31—Library Company of Philadelphia (kitchen); Colonial Williamsburg Foundation (sampler); p. 32—Corbis/Michael Boys; p. 33—Early Music Shop (French horn); Corbis/Arne Hodalic; p. 34—From the book *La Contredance: et les Renouvellements de la Danse Française* by Jean-Michel Guilcher, published by Mouton de Gruyter, Berlin, Germany, used with permission; p. 35—Culver Pictures; pp. 36-38—illustrations by Susan Moore; p. 39—Colonial Williamsburg Foundation; p. 40—Photography by Jamie Young, Prop Styling by Jean doPico.

TABLE OF CONTENTS

FELICITY'S FAMILY

FATHER
Felicity's father, who owns one of the general stores in Williamsburg.

MOTHER
Felicity's mother, who takes care of her family with love and pride.

FELICITY
A spunky, spritely colonial girl, growing up just before the American Revolution.

NAN
Felicity's sweet and sensible sister, who is seven years old.

WILLIAM
*Felicity's three-year-old
brother, who likes mischief
and mud puddles.*

MISS MANDERLY
*Felicity's teacher—
a gracious gentlewoman.*

ELIZABETH COLE
Felicity's best friend.

ANNABELLE COLE
*Elizabeth's snobby
elder sister.*

FELICITY'S
DANCING SHOES

Felicity Merriman ran up the steps of Miss Manderly's house and rushed inside. She was quite wet from running through the rain, so she shook the water off her petticoats before she went into the parlor and sat next to her friend Elizabeth.

"My goodness!" exclaimed Annabelle, Elizabeth's elder sister. "You look as if you were blown here by a hurricane!" She stared at Felicity's messy

hair and touched her own perfect curls.
"I'm glad my hair doesn't look like a
scrub mop."

"My hair is just a bit wet," Felicity
said crossly. She straightened her cap
and frowned. Every day
Annabelle found *something*
mean to say about Felicity.
She criticized her hair, her dress,
her voice, or her manners.

Elizabeth squeezed Felicity's hand.
"Don't let old Annabelle Bananabelle
bother you," she whispered. But Felicity
couldn't help feeling angry.

"Young ladies," said Miss Manderly.
"We will begin today with a dancing
lesson. Elizabeth, you will be my partner.

Annabelle, you will dance with Felicity."

Felicity sighed, and Elizabeth gave her a look full of understanding. It was always dreadful to be the one who had to dance with Annabelle. But Felicity knew the sad truth—she was not a good dancer with *any* partner. No matter how hard she tried, she could not seem to remember how one step led to another. Annabelle always found a great deal to say about her dancing.

Felicity took her place next to Annabelle and nervously watched Miss Manderly demonstrate the dance steps.

"Stay light on your feet," Miss Manderly said. "Do as I do. Gracefully, young ladies!"

Felicity struggled to follow Miss Manderly's directions, but her feet would not cooperate. They wandered off in wrong directions and tangled themselves up.

Annabelle was no help. She sank down when Felicity rose up. She stepped forward when Felicity stepped back. She hopped before Felicity did and turned after Felicity did. She hissed directions. "No! Step back!" she whispered fiercely.

Felicity made more and more mistakes. At one point she lost her balance, fell toward Annabelle, and *bump!* smashed right into her. Felicity's nose banged into Annabelle's shoulder and her foot landed with a thud on Annabelle's toe.

"Ouch! My toe! Oh, my toe!" screeched Annabelle. "You've stepped on my toe, you clumsy girl!" Moaning, Annabelle grabbed her foot in both hands and fell back into a chair.

"I'm sorry," Felicity apologized. "I didn't . . ."

"'Tis no wonder my toe is crushed,"
Annabelle fussed. "You always wear
those dreadful shoes!"

Everyone looked down at Felicity's
feet. Usually, Felicity did not give her
shoes a moment's thought. But now that
Annabelle had drawn attention to them,
Felicity was ashamed. Her everyday
shoes looked scuffed, ugly, and big.
Compared with the dainty shoes
Annabelle and Elizabeth wore, Felicity's
shoes looked as heavy as horseshoes.

"I don't suppose you have any
proper shoes to wear," sniffed
Annabelle.

"Annabelle! That will
do," said Miss Manderly

firmly. "Felicity has apologized, and I am sure she will be more careful in the future. Practice will help her. 'Tis no matter how clumsy one's shoes are. Gracefulness is in the foot, not the shoe."

Annabelle flashed Felicity a satisfied smirk. They'd both heard Miss Manderly call Felicity's shoes clumsy.

Suddenly Felicity was filled with fury. *That Annabelle!* she thought. *She always humiliates me! I'll show her! Somehow, I shall get some dainty shoes. Annabelle won't embarrass me again!*

Felicity's younger sister, Nan, was waiting for her when she got home. As usual, Nan was full of curiosity about lessons. "Lissie," she asked eagerly, "did Miss Manderly teach you a new dance today?"

"Aye, she did," said Felicity dully as she put on her apron. Nan *always* asked about dancing. She loved it as much as Felicity hated it.

"Oh! Please, Lissie, will you teach me the dance?" Nan begged. "Please?"

Suddenly Felicity had an idea. She smiled. Perhaps she had found a way to have the dainty shoes she wanted! "I'd be glad to teach you the dance, Nan," she said. "It's a dandy one. But I must ask you to do me a favor in return."

"A favor?" asked Nan.

"Aye," said Felicity. "I will teach you all the dances Miss Manderly teaches me if you will let me borrow your brocade shoes for lessons from now on."

Nan tilted her head and asked, "Do you mean my brocade shoes like the ones you had until you ruined them?"

"Yes," said Felicity quickly. She might have known Nan would remember that. "But I won't ruin yours. I promise."

Nan was cautious. "Well . . . " she said.

"Of course, if you don't want to learn the dances, you needn't lend me the shoes," said Felicity lightly, as if she did not care.

9

"Oh, but I *do* want to learn the dances," said Nan. She hurried to fetch the shoes from the clothes press and give them to Felicity. "Won't they be too small for you?"

"Not at all," said Felicity, sounding more sure than she was. She kicked off her heavy shoes and tried to fit her right foot into one of Nan's dainty shoes. It was too narrow and much too short, but Felicity did not give up. She pulled very hard on the back of the shoe, wiggled her foot, and bent her toes. Finally, she squeezed her heel inside. "There!" she said, a little out of breath. "You see? I have only to bend my toes a bit and it fits perfectly."

Nan looked doubtful. "But will you be able to dance?" she asked.

"Of course!" answered Felicity. She stood. Her foot was uncomfortable in the tight shoe, but she smiled at Nan anyway. "I think perhaps I will wear my old shoes while I teach you," she said. "It won't do to wear out yours."

When Felicity went to her lessons the next afternoon, she carried Nan's shoes hidden in a cloth bag. Felicity and Nan had agreed not to tell Mother about their arrangement. It just wasn't the sort of thing Mother would approve of.

Once at Miss Manderly's, Felicity slipped into the garden shed. She put her heavy shoes in the bag and hid the bag in a basket under some gardening tools. It looked as if no one had used the tools in a long time. Then she sat on the bench and struggled to pull on Nan's shoes. The brocade made ripping noises, but Felicity ignored them. With her feet squeezed into the dainty shoes, Felicity walked, painfully but proudly, into Miss Manderly's house.

"Oh, Lissie! How pretty!" exclaimed Elizabeth when she saw Felicity's new shoes.

Annabelle just snorted. *Good!* Felicity thought. *Old Annabelle Bananabelle can find nothing mean to say today!*

While Felicity was seated, the shoes were not *too* uncomfortable, though her feet tingled as if they were being pricked with needles and pins. When she stood for the dance lesson, however, the shoes pinched her toes badly. Felicity tried not to think about the pain. She was very careful during dance lessons and made far fewer mistakes than usual.

Miss Manderly smiled with approval.

"Lissie!" said Elizabeth softly, in the middle of a curtsy. "Your new shoes make such a difference in your dancing! They're magic!"

"Indeed they are," Felicity agreed happily. She was delighted with her magic new shoes.

After lessons, back in the gardener's shed, Felicity quickly peeled off the brocade shoes, put them in the bag, and hid the bag under the tools in the basket. She wiggled her toes and rubbed her cramped and weary feet all over. Her old shoes felt as big as boats when she put them on. *Gracious!* thought Felicity. *No one could dance gracefully in these!*

"Very good, Felicity!" said
Miss Manderly a few weeks later. "Your
dancing has certainly improved."

Felicity and Elizabeth exchanged
a smile. They knew that the secret of
Felicity's improvement was in her new
shoes. Ever since Felicity had started
to wear them, her dancing had become
better and better. Even Annabelle had
stopped making mean comments about it.

Sometimes it seemed to Felicity that
the shoes were getting smaller every day,
because every day they hurt more. But
whenever she thought about returning
to her old shoes, she remembered how
Annabelle had humiliated her. Squeezed

feet were less painful than hurt pride.

Nan never let Felicity forget her promise to teach her dancing in return for wearing the brocade shoes. Every day, when Felicity came home from Miss Manderly's, Nan was waiting for her. "Time for my dance lesson!" she'd say cheerfully. And Felicity would have to repeat the dance lesson step by step.

Nan was a fussy student. "Show me exactly how Miss Manderly did it," she'd say. Nan wanted to know every detail of the dance, every step and hop and turn. Felicity had to memorize all Miss Manderly's movements. Nan could always tell when Felicity was just making something up because she had forgotten the real steps. Nan was very careful. She made Felicity go over and over the dance until she was sure she had it right.

With Nan, Felicity danced in her stocking feet. She wouldn't dream of dancing in her heavy shoes, even though mistakes didn't matter so much at home since Annabelle wasn't there to point them out loudly. Indeed, Felicity began to think that dancing with Nan was *almost* fun.

One afternoon, Miss Manderly taught the girls a particularly long and complicated dance. Afterward, Felicity limped her way to the garden shed. She collapsed on the bench, sighed in relief, and looked around for the garden basket containing her old shoes. In an instant, her relief turned to panic. The basket was gone! Her old shoes were gone! They'd disappeared!

Frantically, Felicity searched the tiny shed. Where could the basket be? She

looked under flowerpots and buckets.
She looked on shelves and in corners.
She looked behind watering cans, rakes,
and hoes. The basket was nowhere
to be seen. She rushed outside
the shed and began to search
behind bushes and trees.
What shall I do? she thought.
*Mother will be furious if I've lost my old
shoes. And if I have to wear these pinching
shoes all the time, I shall die! I have to find
that basket!*

Felicity was on her hands and knees,
looking under a garden bench, when she
heard Miss Manderly call to her from the
window, "Gracious, Felicity! What are
you doing?"

"Miss Manderly," Felicity cried. "Where is your garden basket with the tools in it?"

Miss Manderly looked surprised. "My garden basket?" she said. "I suppose Mr. Halibut the gardener came to pick it up today. He said he'd come fetch the tools to clean them before he put them away for the winter. But . . ."

"Mr. Halibut!" exclaimed Felicity, jumping up. "Where did he go?"

"He gardens for the Milners, too, on Francis Street," said Miss Manderly, still confused.

"Thank you, Miss Manderly," said Felicity. And with that, she took off at a run.

Ah, but she had forgotten that she was still wearing Nan's shoes! Running in the little shoes was even more painful than dancing in them. Felicity felt as if knives were stabbing her in the foot with each step. She could also feel a nasty blister forming on one heel. She hadn't gone far before she couldn't stand it any longer. Though the ground was cold and muddy, Felicity tugged off Nan's shoes and shoved them in her pockets.

Felicity could actually run faster without the shoes. She ran past shops and houses, darted around carriages and carts, and ducked through gates and under hedges until she reached Francis Street. She hurried around to the back of

the Milners' house just in time to see Mr. Halibut leaving. He had Miss Manderly's basket over his arm.

"Mr. Halibut, sir," Felicity cried, all in a fluster. "I've left a basket in your bag. I mean a bag in your basket. It's got my shoes in it. The bag does. Please, may I have it back?"

Mr. Halibut looked surprised. He
held the basket out to Felicity without
saying a word. Quickly, she took out
the bag.

"Thank you, Mr. Halibut," she said.
She clutched the bag to her chest and
headed home. She could not put her
shoes on because her stockings were wet
and filthy. Her poor bruised feet were
numb with cold anyway. And so she
stumbled along in her stocking feet.

The next day Felicity plodded off to
lessons in her old shoes. As soon as she'd
come home the day before and Mother
had seen her ruined stockings, she had

had to confess the whole long story.

"Felicity," Mother had said firmly. "This nonsense will stop. You may no longer borrow Nan's shoes."

Now Felicity's heart was as heavy as her old shoes. She knew her dancing would be just as it had been before. She would be clumsy, and Annabelle would gleefully call attention to all her mistakes.

In fact, Annabelle did not even wait for the dance lesson to begin before she said something mean. "Gracious me!" she said loudly. "You're wearing those dreadful shoes again! We must all look out for our toes!"

Felicity was not surprised.

But everyone—even Annabelle—*was*

surprised when the lesson began. Felicity was not clumsy at all! She was light on her feet! She was graceful! Her old black shoes flew through the dance without a single mistake.

"You're dancing so well!" whispered Elizabeth, delighted. "I guess the magic was not in the new shoes after all!"

Felicity laughed. Suddenly she knew what the real magic *was.* Without realizing it, she had been practicing her dancing every day when she gave Nan her lessons. It was the practice that had made the difference in her dancing, not magic shoes. She had suffered the pain of the pinching shoes for no reason. What a joke she had played on herself!

"Well, Elizabeth," she said to her friend happily. "After all, gracefulness is in the foot, not the shoe."

VALERIE TRIPP

At 9   Now

When I took dancing lessons, I was taller than all the boys in my class. That meant I usually had to dance with the teacher, which was embarrassing. But at least he was the best dancer in the class!

Valerie Tripp has written twenty-nine books in The American Girls Collection, including eight about Felicity.

LOOKING
BACK
1774

A PEEK INTO
THE PAST

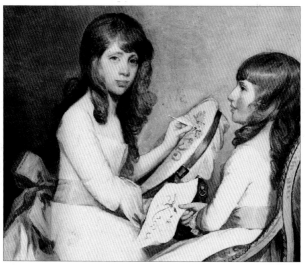

Girls like Felicity spent most of their days learning how to become proper gentlewomen. Their mothers taught them how to direct the activities of the household so that one day they could direct their own servants and slaves. Girls learned how to prepare meals, make and mend clothes, preserve meats, and dry herbs for cooking and medicine. They also learned how to plant a proper garden with

Girls learned how to cook and to stitch fancy samplers.

herbs near the kitchen house and sweet-smelling flowers near the main house.

Colonial girls were also expected to learn the art of being a lady. President Thomas Jefferson wrote to his daughter, "Follow closely your music, reading, sewing, housekeeping." Teachers like Miss Manderly taught girls how to write elegantly and to create samplers of fancy stitchery. Girls also practiced singing and playing musical instruments. Most girls learned

Harpsichord

to play the
spinet or the
harpsichord,
a pianolike
instrument,
as well as the
guitar. Girls
would never have

French horn

Violin

played the French horn or violin.
Colonial gentlefolk thought it ungraceful
for a young lady to bend her neck or
pucker her lips!

Above all, girls learned how to
dance. In the southern colonies, dance
lessons were a very important part of a
wealthy young lady's education. From
about the age of eight, girls took as many

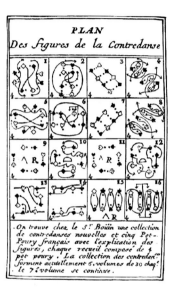

Dance diagram

as nine hours of dance classes a week. They practiced at home, too, using books that *diagrammed,* or drew out, the dance steps.

Dancing was supposed to help girls with their *deportment,* or posture and grace while moving. They learned the proper way to curtsy and memorized the steps to many difficult routines. It was easy to get flustered, but practice made

perfect, just as
Felicity found out.
And girls practiced
especially hard
when they heard
a dance master
was coming
to town.

Throughout the southern colonies, dance masters traveled from plantation to plantation to give special dance lessons. These masters watched every move their students made. They were known to be quite strict! After one lesson, a student wrote in his diary that the master had "struck two girls for faults in the course of their performance, even in the presence of the mother of one of them."

All the hard work seemed worth it, however, when a girl was old enough to attend her first ball. A ball was a social event not to be missed! It was a chance for young ladies and gentlemen to meet, and perhaps even steal a minute alone.

 A ball began with an elegant meal late in the afternoon. Then the dancing started, with the stately *minuet* (min-yoo-WET). This was the most important dance of all. Only one couple at a time performed, while all the other guests watched. It was a girl's chance to

"show herself to the best advantage."

The minuet began with *honors,* or a polite bow and curtsy. Then a girl balanced on the ball of one foot, spun around gracefully while still holding her partner's hand, and stepped carefully with pointed toes in perfect time to the music.

Throughout the evening, the music at a ball became more lively and the dancing more relaxed. Partners joined together to perform circle dances like reels and

jigs that could last
until early the
next morning.
Often, many
guests would
return in the after-
noon for a second
day of dancing!

In the northern colonies, such
behavior would have been considered
shocking. There, many people
thought dancing was
"wicked," just like drinking
or playing cards.

Over time, however, dancing became
accepted throughout the colonies. Still, it
was only in the south that a host would

be dismayed when her guests wanted to leave after only six days of dancing!

An evening of colonial music and dancing

AN
AMERICAN
GIRLS
PASTIME

A
LITTLE KEYBOARD BOOK

Eight Tunes of Colonial Virginia
Set for Piano or Harpsichord
by
J. S. Darling

TRY COLONIAL SQUARE DANCING

Take a dancing lesson!

Felicity was thrilled when she realized that she really could dance—and dance well! All it took was a lot of practice and patience. You can learn some of the same dance steps Felicity did. Gather your friends, and pretend you are attending your very own dance lesson.

YOU WILL NEED:

Classical music from the 1700s*
A friend to dance with

*Music by J. C. Bach, Handel, or Mozart,
available in libraries or music stores. Or sing
"Yankee Doodle Dandy," which was
popular during the Revolution.

First, perform a proper curtsy.

1. Stand with your back straight and your arms at your sides. Place one foot a little in front of the other.

2. Slightly bow your head and tilt it a bit to the side. Make sure your eyes are looking down.

3. Sink down slowly, pause, and then rise. Don't sink too low or rise too fast. You'll lose your balance!

Now try the minuet.

1. Stand next to your partner and hold her hand. Walk forward together—left, right, left. Stop and point your right toes out in front of you. Walk forward again, starting with your right feet.

2. Face your partner and hold hands. Step onto your left feet and swing your right feet forward. Then step onto your right feet and swing your left feet forward.

3. One partner lets go with her right hand, raises her left arm, and twirls her partner under her arm.

4. Repeat steps 1 to 3. Once you have the steps down, repeat them to music.

THE AMERICAN GIRLS COLLECTION®

To learn more about The American Girls Collection, fill out the postcard
below and mail it to American Girl, or call **1-800-845-0005**. We'll send you
a free catalogue full of books, dolls, dresses, and other delights for girls.
You can also visit our Web site at **www.americangirl.com**.

**I'm an American girl who loves to get mail. Please send
me a catalogue of The American Girls Collection:**

My name is _____

My address is _____

City _____ State _____ Zip _____

My birth date is ___/___/___ Parent's signature _____
         Month Day Year

And send a catalogue to my friend:

My friend's name is _____

Address _____

City _____ State _____ Zip _____

1961

1225